From A Thug to A Saint

Fredrick D. Mason

From a Thug to a Saint

Published by Hadassah's Crown Publishing, LLC
634 NE Main St #1263
Simpsonville, SC 29681

ISBN: 979-8-9923918-0-0

Printed in the United States

Contents

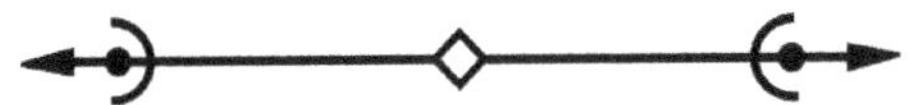

Chapter 1:

Pen ur Pal

"Mail call," the male prison guard called out to the men in the barracks as he was working.

"Keith Rogers, mail call. Do you want me to grab it for you?" asked Lil Peanut.

"Yeah!" Keith said as he continued to roll the marijuana joint while sitting on his prison bunk.

Lil Peanut was excited for Keith. Keith had been waiting on a response from a female he had met through a new pen pal service named "Pen-Ur-Pal." He hoped Keith received some pictures of this female he'd talked so much about. He was anxious to see the female, too.

"Big bro, do you mind if I open your letter just to see if there's some flix in it?" Lil Peanut laughed, but he was really being serious.

Keith looked up from getting a spark from the two AA batteries he was using to fire up the marijuana joint. "Boy you play too much. Nigga give me my mail!" as he snatched it from his hand while he passed the joint to Lil Peanut.

"My boy! This is from ol' girl," said a smiling Keith.

"I know already," Lil Peanut said, as he took another toke from the marijuana joint.

Keith didn't pay him no mind. His focus was on getting to his mail. He had been expecting a response from LaSonya. Her letter couldn't have come at a better time.

"Let me hit that one more time before I lay back," he said, reaching to grab half of the joint.

"Bruh, that some fire bud. These niggas going to love that shit. What a gram of that going for?"

"Fifty a gram."

"You know that bud taste like some Gorilla Glue," Lil Peanut said while tasting the bud sitting on his tongue.

"You absolutely right. That's Gorilla Glue. My family be copping that shit by the bales. My boy, I told you once I walk out this prison, I am connected with whatever I need. And that's on my real momma."

They both fell over laughing, as the weed affected their mindsets. Lil Peanut knew Keith was being honest. Everything he'd said was usually legit. As Lil Peanut walked away from Keith's bunk, Keith laid back with his penitentiary tablet and CL20 headphones listening to his slow jams playlist. He opened his letter from LaSonya.

Saturday, May 27, 2023

Dear Keith,

Hello, man of the hour. I truly hope this well-expected letter brings a smile not only to your face but to your heart as well. Before this letter goes any further, I would like you to know that your words of encouragement were very intriguing. Your words really place me somewhere other than Atlanta, Georgia. Everything you wrote replenished the emptiness that I've lived with for some time now. I admire your peaceful spirit. It's breathtaking. I assure you I can get used to it.

You mention in your letter that you weren't a believer of God. Well, that's interesting. I am not here to judge you or your beliefs. But I will say if you only allow Him to entertain your thoughts, heart, and mind for a moment, your whole life will change. And again, I am not trying to push my belief off on you. You also mentioned you are expecting to go before the parole board in less than a year. I'm quite sure you're excited. I will be bringing this before the Lord.

So, you know, I am a strong believer in God's way of life. I am so amazed at the peace and joy He gives to me when I call on Him. When I bring a situation to Him and decree and declare it, my, my, my, it's usually done. And if it's not done in the timing I wanted it done, then more than likely, He's working out something better for me to understand and to enjoy.

So, I said all of that to say, I will be praying over your parole date and the day God opens those gates for you to reintegrate into society. I enclosed some pictures of me. I hope you like them. Really, pictures do not do me any justice. LOL.…. People have their opinion of me on pictures, but I beg to differ. But I am sure you will give me your feedback once you write back. SMHWL!!!

This week, I plan to spend a couple days working with our Outreach Youth Center. I have a big passion for our at-risk teenagers. So, I will be busy. And of course, spend some time with my parents and my American Bully. As you can see as of right now, I am a simple person. I don't need much to be pleased. I hope I have stimulated your mind for now. I leave you as I come, in peace.

Sincerely,

LaSonya G.

Keith laid the letter down and let the words to the music and the effects of the good bud just take him to a place he longed to be for a while now, the free world.

Chapter 2:
Raggedy Childhood

Keith had been in prison for twelve years for second-degree murder. When he entered prison, he didn't have a clue how he was going to make it through. Every day he kept his mind on being successful once he made it back home.

He knew back home he didn't have much to return to. His mother was mentally disturbed now. Someone had slipped her a mickey at the club one night. He never knew his father. His mother would always tell him every time he asked about his dad, that he's in California working. For years, he believed that until one day his older cousin called herself getting mad because Grandma ruled in his favor instead of hers. She yelled out, "Your daddy not in no California. Your daddy is a crack head and he's right around the corner!" From that point on, he always looked throughout the neighborhood for someone who resembled him and someone who could possibly be his father.

Keith was from a small town in Arkansas by the name of Forrest City. He grew up on the southside. The neighborhood he lived in with his mother was raggedy. Everything around them screamed out poverty.

At the age of sixteen, Keith and one of his neighborhood friends watched an older man religiously in the hood as he went backward and forward to this shed in his backyard. One night when the sky fell dark, Keith and Devin creeped through the back alley and jumped the small fence in the man's backyard. Devin had the bold cutters, and Keith had a small flashlight and a 380 handgun, just in case things didn't go according to their plans.

Once Devin cut the lock off, it was downhill from there. Keith didn't want to get caught slipping, so he stayed on guard while Devin went in to see what had the old man running back and forth. Devin wasn't in the shed long before he said, "My boy, I think we just scored big!"

Being anxious to know what he was meaning, he stepped inside to get a glance of what had Devin so excited.

"Oh shit! Is that weed and money?" asked Keith.

"You better know it," Devin said as he didn't waste any time by filling the pounds of marijuana in a garbage bag. "Go ahead and do your thing with filling up these bags. I am going to get back on post. But hurry up, we don't got long."

Devin moved as fast as he could. He tried to get every pound of marijuana that was sitting along the shelf along the wall. Inside a trash bag filled with cash sat in the corner of the small shed. As he brought the bag filled with weed out, he looked up at Keith and smiled. He went back in and grabbed the bag of money. They both knew their lives were about to change tremendously. As they made it back over the small fence, they saw the back porch light pop on. They both knew if someone were after them, then it was too late.

Keith knew he couldn't go to his house because his grandmother and his mother were still there, probably still up watching their favorite TV series *The Wire*. So, they both went over to Devin's house. Getting everything counted, the money added up to a total amount of $180,000 and six pounds of weed. They split everything fifty-fifty. But they made a promise to one another to not go out and spend big. They would keep everything on the low for a while.

Chapter 3:

Rags to Riches

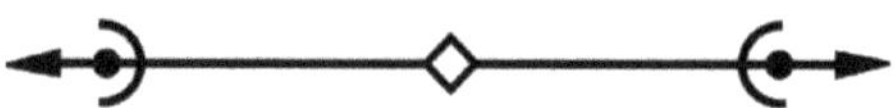

One month and a half later…

Keith had heard from friends in the neighborhood that Old Man Wallace had put out a $5000 reward to anyone with valuable information about who broke into his storage. Keith knew he had been careful since robbing the old man. He had not been spending, but Devin on the other hand, had purchased a cash two-door Cutlass. It's true the car was nothing fancy, but Keith knew they needed no attention brought their way.

One day, Keith and Devin walked into Coleman's Barber Shop that sat on the top corner of South Division and Day Street. Ever since they could remember, if you wanted to know about the latest gossip, you could go to Coleman's and find out anything and everything.

Barber Johnny J's chair had just come available when Keith walked through the door. By having Keith in his chair, Johnny J knew he was good for a nice sizable tip. Devin took a seat in one of the waiting area chairs. His barber had a customer in his chair.

"Did y'all hear about Pastor Phillip Goodman, AKA Pastor Feel Good, being caught by his wife coming out of Sister Janice's house the other day?" Fat Freddy asked, as he sucked on an already clean chicken bone.

"Man, don't put no bad jacket on my pastor," said another old man, who was waiting in line for a haircut.

"Deacon Curtis, I hate to be the one to tell you, but yo Pastor is a hoe," said Fat Freddy with a straight face. The entire barbershop burst into laughter.

"Fat Freddy, will you leave a man of God alone?" asked Johnny J.

"Okay. I will do just that. But somebody need to tell Pastor Feel Good he needs to leave his church members alone."

Again, the barbershop was rolling. Deacon Curtis stood to his feet and stormed out of the shop.

"Now Fat Freddy, you can't be running my business away," said Johnny J.

"Hell, I can't help it if I am telling the God honest truth. If he didn't want to hear it, hell, he shouldn't have came in here today."

The barbershop fell silent for a brief moment until Old Man Wallace walked in.

"What's up, old timer?" asked Poppa Smurf, another middle-age guy who waited in the barbershop for his usual shave and line.

"Ah, nothing too much," Wallace said as he walked over to Poppa Smurf, giving him some dap.

"What have you been up to here lately?" asked Poppa Smurf.

"Really been laying low, while playing slow. Just trying to find out some information about a break-in at my house a little over a month ago."

"Believe it or not, I heard someone mentioning something about some break-ins in the neighborhood. But if someone try to come up into my house, I bet you they don't leave the way they came in."

The people in the shop laughed except Wallace. Fat Freddy had to put his two cents in everything.

"I think I heard something about that," said Fat Freddy, who was still chewing on another piece of chicken bone.

The anxious listeners, including Keith and Devin, wanted to know what information he had to share. "My brother-in-law, who live maybe two houses down diagonal of your house, said he was standing out on his back porch when he seen two males jumping your fence and heading east up the dark alley."

Keith and Devin both looked at one another, and they both looked back at Old Man Wallace who didn't look too old up close and in person. He appeared to be in his late forties and had a scar across his right jaw line.

"Do you mind if I speak to this brother-in-law of yours?" asked Wallace with interest.

"Well, you know he's a Christian and don't like to get in nobody business."

Before Fat Freddy could finish his statement, Wallace was coming out of his pocket with a fist full of one-hundred-dollar bills. Peeling one off and handing it to Fat Freddy, he said, "I honestly don't think he would mind if you came by there. He don't have company that much. He stays on Day Street in the white house with a flower pot on the front porch and a white GMC pick-up truck in the driveway."

"Thanks for the information," Wallace said, as he looked around the barbershop, furious at the thought of someone trying to play him weak.

Chapter 4:
Old Gangsta

As the next couple of weeks passed, Keith and Devin laid low with their spending. They both tried their best to keep an eye on Old Man Wallace. They realized that he was determined to find out who robbed his storage. The barbershop incident clarified that for them both.

Wallace rode the neighborhood streets religiously while passing out money to any and everybody he thought could give him information on who robbed his storage. He had moved from Chicago six years earlier after he had to put down a mean demonstration that caused two stupid old heads their lives. He thought by coming down to a slow country town that he'd be able to lay back, mess with the ladies and make a bunch of money from the bud connection he had.

Chapter 5:
House Party

Keith and Devin were attending a neighborhood house party a couple sisters on Church Street were having. Sherita and Takisha were some fine females, but they were freaks, though. There weren't too many dudes in their neighborhoods and other hoods who didn't hit them both. But for the most part, they were some cool chicks, and Keith and Devin knew there were going to be some hot honeys at the party.

When both of the good-looking brothers walked in, Takisha hugged Devin and smiled at Keith. Devin had been seeing her on the low and thought no one in the hood knew. One thing about the Southside, nothing happened that someone didn't already know by morning or night fall.

"Devin, did you bring some of that good bud you smoked with us two nights ago?" asked Takisha, as she looked up at him while blinking her long eyelashes.

Devin went in his Polo jacket pocket and pulled out what could have been an ounce of King Kong bud. Keith looked upside his head as if he was crazy. One thing Keith knew about situations like this was that any time you bring out some bud at a party, you'll become the man of the party, or at least until it runs out. At that very moment, all attention was on Devin and his big bag of bud.

As the party continued, people started to really liven up. The bud smoke was in the air. People started dancing, drinking more and several couples dipped off to the other part of the house. Keith had this short, thick, chocolate girl jammed up by the kitchen. He was trying to enjoy himself, but something about the bud Devin pulled out really didn't sit well with him. So, he kept an eye on his boy.

"This bud taste just like Old Man Wallace bud," the two females were saying, as they both passed Keith coming out of the kitchen while puffing on the freshly rolled blunt. He cut his macking short and pushed way over to Devin and told him they needed to get out of there and fast. Devin saw the serious look on Keith's face and knew something wasn't right.

Chapter 6:
Cool, Calm, and Collective

The following morning, Keith walked to the corner store for his grandmother. She needed her BC powder for her headache and some cornstarch. She also had other items on her list, but those two things she couldn't go a day without. After Keith gathered his sack from the cash register and was exiting the store, Old Man Wallace was heading toward the store entrance.

"Say youngblood, I've seen you and your partner around the neighborhood a few times. Have y'all seen two young cats with a large sum of bud and cash?" he asked, while handing Keith a big face Benjamin Franklin.

Keith extended his hand, accepted the money and politely said, "No, I haven't, but if I do, I will be sure to let you know. Because I could sure use that bread you have as the reward."

Keith walked off as calmly and as cool as he possibly could. His mind was set on only two things, getting his boy Devin and thinking of his next move. Because he knew as smoothly as Old Man Wallace spoke, this old timer wasn't a fool.

Chapter 7:
Wise Soul

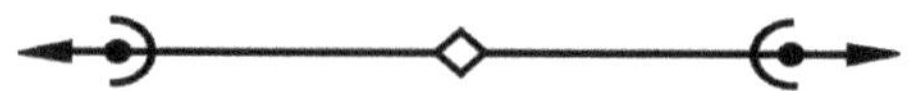

When Keith walked back into his grandmother's house, he wore a puzzled look on his face. This alerted his grandmother that something was wrong, and she needed to know what she could do about it.

"Grandson, is something troubling you?"

"No ma'am," Keith said, lying while removing his jacket and laying it across the kitchen chair.

"Baby, you know your granny knows everything, and especially when it comes to my apple-headed grandson, who I've raised basically since birth. Now tell Grandma what's the matter," she said, rubbing Keith's tight fade.

Keith made up another lie to downplay what his grandmother had already suspected about what was troubling him. Mom Dukes had raised a daughter, which was Keith's mother who was still living wild. She had two sons who fell victim to the street life that claimed their lives in a home invasion, twelve years before Keith was born.

Grandmother knew her stubborn baby boy was hiding something from her. She just knew to do the only next best thing, and that was to take it to the Lord in prayer.

"Keith, when was the last time you and your big-headed friend Devin been to church?"

He knew his granny asked questions that she already knew the answer to. "It's been a while." He knew where this question was leading to. But he knew better than to interrupt her line of questions.

"God spoke to me about you and Devin last night."

"Is that right, Granny?" asked Keith, as he made his way to the refrigerator.

"Son, I don't want to sound like I am preaching at you, but I need for you to slow down. I may not be out here with you, but my God speaks to me. I have a personal connection with Him."

As Keith raised up from looking in the fridge, he looked her in the eyes and said, "Mom Dukes, I don't think you heard me. But everything is okay. You have nothing to worry about when it comes to me or big-headed Devin. We're good," he said as he grabbed both of her hands.

"Well, since you just assured me that everything is all good, then make plans for tomorrow morning to go with me to church. You and that big head boy Devin," said Mom Dukes, as she whisked eggs in a mixing bowl.

Keith knew he had to agree, if he wanted to get her off his back. "Yes ma'am, I will. We will be there bright and early."

"Because what?" Mom Dukes said for Keith to finish his sentence.

"You don't like to miss your morning Sunday school."

"That's my boy," Mom Dukes said, as she came over to pat him on his blushing cheek.

Chapter 8:
Avoid Warning

After Keith finished with his morning house chores, he took a stroll around the corner to Devin's house. He knew Devin would be upset because he agreed for him to be up and ready for church Sunday morning. And not just church but Sunday school. The thought of the idea made Keith smile.

As Keith got closer to Devin's house, he noticed two people sitting in his car. Keith walked alongside the driver side window and knocked on the window. Devin let down the window and a cloud of smoke came rushing out. After the smoke cleared, he bent down to see Takisha sitting on the passenger side with the blunt in her hand.

"My boy, do you have a few minutes?" Keith asked Devin.

"Yeah! Get in," Devin said, as he made an attempt to open his door for Keith to get in the backseat.

"No, in private," said a frowning Keith.

"Go ahead and finish that. I will be right back. Let me holler at my boy."

Keith started gradually walking up the street, giving himself a second to cool off and the opportunity to talk privately to his hard-headed boy.

"What's up, bruh?" asked Devin, looking loaded from the good marijuana he had continuously smoked since robbing Old Man Wallace.

"Bruh, is there ever a time when you're not smoking?"

That wasn't a question for Devin to answer, because he knew the answer to it already. Devin didn't even try to muster an answer to that question because he knew every day he'd been on cloud twenty.

"Anyway, what's up."

"I believe Old Man Wallace is on to us."

Devin stopped and rubbed his nine-millimeter handgun he had copped a couple of days ago.

"What brings you to that conclusion?"

"This morning, I was leaving the corner store for Mom Dukes, and he stopped me as I was exiting. He asked if either you or I saw two young cats with a large sum of cash or bud.."

"Ah shit. That old ass nigga just fishing my boy! Just stay on Yo P's and Q's, and this shit will blow over."

"Bruh, you make this shit sound so easy. So, I guess you are laying low and on your square?"

"Keith," as he lifted his shirt to show off his nickel plated 9mm. "It's death on mines."

"Okay, whatever. Just be careful. Oh, another thing."

"What is it now?"

"I've already agreed for both of us to go to church with Mom Dukes tomorrow morning, bright and early."

"Hell naw, Keith!" said a disappointed Devin. He had plans to ride to Memphis, Tennessee, get a hotel room and freak with Takisha all night long.

"Sorry my boy, and by the way, she is expecting us to be there for Sunday school."

"Damn, Keith. You have really messed me around this time," as he walked back to his car while shaking his head.

Keith nor Devin saw Wallace sitting in an unfamiliar car looking through a pair of binoculars at them. He had done his investigation. He knew that by passing out the one-hundred-dollar bills, someone was going to talk. He had heard about the big bag of bud the young nigga Devin had at the party the other night. When he approached the nigga Keith with his line of questions, he had already known what he was going to say. He just wanted to get a good look at him up close before he made his move. He thought his lurking days were over. But he guessed even in the country, they have suckers, too.

Chapter 9:
Deadly Kill

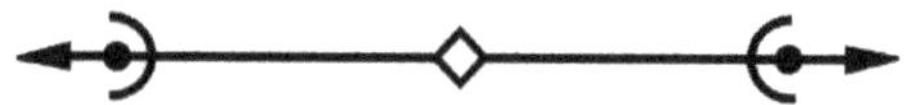

As the daylight escaped, stars filled the clear bright sky. Devin cut his night short, but he knew Mom Dukes would have his head if he wasn't at church on Sunday. He looked over himself in the full-length mirror for the second time as he smoothed down his bee-hived waves. He walked over to his dresser and grabbed a brand-new bottle of Polo Red cologne. He knew the fragrance was going to coincide with the loud smell of marijuana he was sure to smoke all night long.

As Devin made a beeline to the front door, he didn't worry about checking in on his 72-year-old grandfather, because he knew at eight o'clock, he was in the room calling the sheep. Before walking out of the house, Devin cocked his peace-maker and repositioned it in his waistband.

As Devin stepped out on the porch and looked around the neighborhood, he didn't see anyone. He ushered his way down the steps over to his Cutlass. After opening the car door and sinking into the comfortable Ostrich seats, Devin placed the key in the ignition and the car came to life.

As Jeezy's "Let's Get it" screamed through the Fast Gate Speakers, Old Man Wallace jumped up from the backseat floorboard, wrapping his arm around Devin's neck while extending the sharp butterfly knife to Devin's throat.

"Bitch nigga, if you ever reach for your waist line, I am going to gut your punk ass like a hog, right here, right now," Wallace said, as he tightened his grip around Devin's neck. "You young motherfuckers must have thought I was going to lay down and accept a loss?"

"Man, what are you talking about?" asked Devin. He knew he had to play it cool, at least until he could get his hand on his gun.

"Don't try and play me. I've put enough money on these streets to get the information I needed. You and your boy broke into my storage last month."

"Old Man Wallace, you got the wrong two guys!"

Devin didn't know what to do. He just knew if this clown slipped one time, he was going to send him to his maker. Wallace tightened his grip even while poking the sharp knife into Devin's throat.

"My boy, I am from Chi-town, not downtown. Insult someone else."

Devin knew then if he didn't think of something and think quick, he wasn't going to make it out alive.

"Okay, we did rob your storage. I have the money and over half of the bud in the house if you come in with me.

I will get it for you and I promise you, I will never mention a thing about this."

Wallace listened to the young nigga shoot his best sale's pitch he could think of, but he wasn't buying it.

"Peep game, little homie. You both should have done some research on who the fuck I was. You both can have that small shit. You both have bought a first-class ticket to hell," he said as he dragged the knife across Devin's throat, slicing it wide open.

Chapter 10:

Heart-Broken

Keith's grandmother asked if he and Devin wanted to ride to church with her. He declined the offer because he knew if they rode with her, they wouldn't be leaving until the last car was out of the parking lot. That would be at about four in the evening. Luckily, his boy had wheels.

When Keith hit the corner to see if Devin was in his car, he was surprised. He just knew he would have to flip this dude's mattress just to get him out of bed. Once he got closer to Devin's car, he noticed blood on the ground near the car door. He snatched open the driver's door to find his boy with his throat cut. He pushed Devin's shoulder to see if there was hope, but it was too late. He was already dead. What caught Keith's attention was the one-hundred-dollar bill laying in Devin's lap. The single bill had Old Man Wallace's name written all over it. He knew he had to find Old Man Wallace before Old Man Wallace found him.

Chapter 11:
Slipping Counts

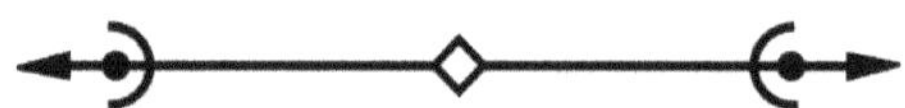

Weeks passed and Old Man Wallace had laid low, hoping to catch Keith slipping. But for the past three weeks, Keith had been out of sight. Wallace had even staked out Devin's funeral just so he could lay eyes on the youngster, but Keith never showed up.

Wallace had figured the mean demonstration he laid down on the youngster had the other country bumpkin thinking twice before his gangster was tested. And he believed it even may have scared that other little nigga away as well. He thought about hurting Keith's pride and joy, his Mom Dukes, just to bring the youngster out of hiding. But he waved that thought off. He didn't want to bring unwanted heat his way.

Chapter 12:
Too Hard to Swallow

Two months had passed and Keith was laying low in Haynes, Arkansas. He was so mad at himself for not taking charge of the situation. He knew they were supposedly already rushed. Old Man Wallace was being persistent about who jacked his storage. But no, they were like sitting ducks, and now his boy was gone.

Once Keith found Devin's lifeless body in the front seat of his car, he broke down and told Mom Dukes what really happened. Mom Dukes tried her best to convince Keith to turn over the drugs and the money to the police to help solve the case. But Keith used his better judgment and lied by saying Devin had it all and he didn't have a clue where it was hidden. Even if she didn't believe him, she didn't question him about it again.

Keith knew he had to go somewhere and fast, because he knew Old Man Wallace was determined to make him out to be the next victim. He knew he couldn't allow that to happen. Devin used to always mention property his grandfather had down in the country. Luckily, he remembered where it was. No one knew Keith's whereabouts. He suffered the first week. He wasn't familiar with well water. There were no utilities in the shotgun house. The only store was in the next town, maybe 15 minutes away.

Keith didn't waste any time before his survival instincts kicked in. He figured if he wanted water, he had to go out back and pump from the well pumps. Once he mastered the well pump, he chopped wood for the fireplace to heat the outdated non-insulated, old house. Keith did what he had to do to survive. He knew his focus had to be sharp when it came to hunting down Old Man Wallace.

As Keith moved throughout the dusty rooms of the small house, he noticed in the far room by the back door that the carpet looked odd. He walked over and bent down to pull the old-fashioned carpet back. A piece of the plank was missing from the board, and it looked as if it were broken purposefully. He lifted the plank and discovered a huge surprise.

Chapter 13:
Coleman's Barber Shop

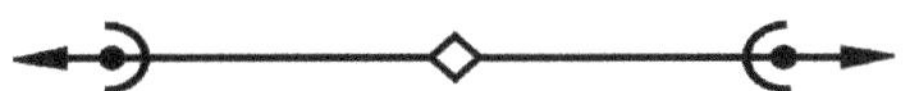

As usual, Fat Freddy was in the shop sitting in his usual chair doing his usual thing, eating and talking.

"Lil Boy, come over here and let me use my clippers to give you a Lil Boostah fade," said Fat Freddy.

The little boy, who may have been ten, hunched his shoulders and walked over to Johnny J's chair.

"Fat Freddy, you will just give someone a name. His name is Jaylon. And his rapper name is Lil Boosie."

"Lil Boosie, Lil Boostah or Lil Bootsie Collins, I was just going to cut that nappy mess off his head and give him that tight fade that boy be wearing."

The little boy rushed over to Johnny J's chair and hopped in, while mean mugging Fat Freddy as if he was crazy. The entire barbershop laughed loudly.

"Have they caught anyone for killing that youngster over on Church Street?" asked Poppa Smurf.

"Not to my knowledge," said Johnny J, as he twirled the barber chair around.

"There's been many rumors going around," said Fat Freddy, while picking his miniature afro.

"Like what?" asked a nosey Poppa Smurf.

"They say that old fellow Wallace had something to do with his killing. But don't no one know that for sure."

"By the way, his boy Lil Keith hasn't been to the shop in a couple months. That's odd for him. He's normally keeping his haircut appointments. He like clockwork," said Johnny J, as he put the finishing touches on the young man's nappy 'fro.

"So do y'all think those two youngsters were the ones burglarizing the neighborhood?" asked Poppa Smurf.

"What I've came to a conclusion about," Fat Freddy said, stuffing the glazed donut down his fat throat, "That those two were the ones who broke into that old fellow storage behind his house."

"How can you be so sure, Fat Freddy? You could easily be putting a rumor out. And that's not nice to do," said Johnny J.

Johnny J. had been around the two boys their entire lives. He grew up on the Southside. There were not too many people he didn't know. But he knew if this was true what Fat Freddy was saying, then it could be bad.

"I have this little fast tail niece that love to be at somebody party. I heard her talking about that boy Devin having the same kind of reefer Old Man Wallace had been selling at a party her and her friends had attended. She said he pulled out a pound and was passing it out to whoever wanted to smoke. Now you tell me, if they didn't or did have something to do with the break-in," said Fat Freddy, really not looking for an answer to his question.

Nobody said a word. Everybody was puzzled by the thought of the young teenager losing his life over something as petty as some marijuana and a little money.

Chapter 14:
Grind Time

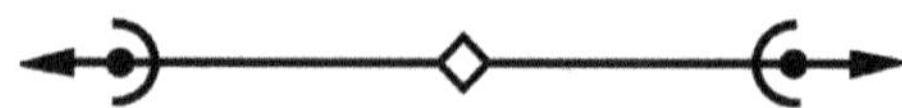

Old Man Wallace was back on the grind as he was before. Business had picked up. He had learned from his past mistake and purchased the house three doors down from his house. He had made that house his stash house. He knew if he wanted to be ahead of the game, he had to do some things differently.

Three months had passed, and he still hadn't spotted the other youngster who made it off with his stash. Every now and then, he would post up and watch the kid's grandmother's house, hoping he would get lucky and spot him coming or going. But for the past three months, there had been no sign of him.

Word was out that Wallace had something to do with Devin's murder, but no one was sure. The only thing they did know was that Keith had disappeared. No one had seen him. And when anyone asked Mom Dukes, she was quick to say she hadn't seen him. Then she'd say, "But I do know he's in God's hands."

Chapter 15:
Keith's Lurkin'

Keith knew if he was going to get revenge on Old Man Wallace, he had to come correct and with full force. He knew he couldn't come half-stepping. So, for days and nights, he sat at the kitchen table playing chess and strategizing a bulletproof plan that would whip Old Man Wallace off the face of the earth. He wanted to know how his mom and Mom Dukes were doing. This was his first time ever being away from them both this long. He knew he had to make a move and make it fast if he wanted to get back to living his life.

Thoughts of his best friend Devin surfaced in his mind daily. He wore Devin's death on his shoulders every single day. For days, he had questioned his loyalty to his best friend. He felt he was the mature one and was supposed to attack first on Old Man Wallace. But instead, he was caught slipping. Keith had made a vow to himself and to Devin by the end of the year that they wouldn't be gangsters pushing up daisies.

Keith took a walk outside for some fresh air. As he started walking up the gravel road, a truck was coming up behind him at a slow and steady speed. He wasn't worried about anyone being there to harm him, because everybody who stayed down in the country minded their own business. He moved over to the side as the truck came closer. The truck came to a stop, and the driver rolled down the window.

"Mr. Handsome, you might want to move over there on that grass before you get yourself ran over," a cute but country, freckled-face white girl said, while smiling at Keith.

"I don't believe you would hit me on purpose, would you?" asked Keith.

"Of course not!"

'That's good to know. But where are you headed?"

"I'm headed to town. Do you need a ride somewhere?" asked the freckled-faced white girl. She was so anxious to be around a black man. Not that she was racist. It was just that during her entire high school years, she found every black dude attractive. But there was always a black chick around who ended up with him. So, she wasn't about to miss this opportunity for nothing.

"When you say town, where are you meaning?" asked a curious Keith.

"Marianna. But if you need to go into Forest City, we could go."

"No, we could go to Marianna."

As Keith walked around the front of the dusty Ford truck and got in on the passenger side, he said, "Oh, by the way, I'm Keith." He extended his hand.

"Nice to meet you, Keith. My name is April," she said, as she welcomed his hand with a pleasant handshake.

"Before we leave, do I have to worry about a big, country-ass white boy rushing me from behind because I'm riding in the truck with you?" Keith was dead ass serious. He didn't need any more unwanted problems. He knew he had enough already.

"You're funny too. But no. You don't have to worry about a big, country-ass white boy tackling you from behind over my white ass. And for your information, I don't date white boys. You know what they say about white boys," April said, while rolling her neck as a sister would do if she were expressing herself.

"And what do they say about a white boy?"

"That they're not packing like a black boy," she said as she looked down towards Keiths' crotch.

They both started laughing. And they went to a dollar store and to KFC. Keith needed a hot meal. He was tired of eating cold-cut sandwiches from the corner store in that small town.

Chapter 16:
Mission at Hand

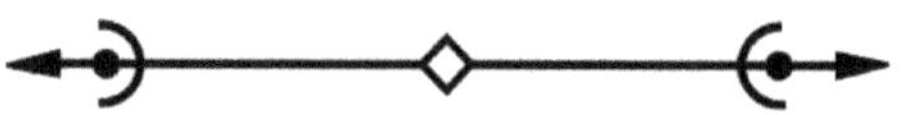

Keith walked back into the house with two shopping bags. Inside the shopping bags were duct tape, a utility rope, black gloves, a black backpack, black dickies, gloves, and a pair of black boots. He knew the mission he was sure to make; he knew it had to be a successful one. April tried her best to talk her way into the shotgun house. But he knew better than to mix business and pleasure. He was focused on one thing, and that was getting revenge. Anything else came second. He was well aware of the mission he was on and who he was dealing with. He hoped he could convince April to secure one of her father's guns. He knew he needed more fire power. She assured him that she would see what she could do. He really wasn't sure what he was going to do about an extra weapon. But he knew he had to do something fast.

Chapter 17:
Gun Talk

April determined how she was going to get next to Keith. She knew he needed a pistol, and it seemed urgent. She knew if she managed to sneak one or maybe two of her father's guns from his gun case, she might get lucky and be able to sample his manly tool. She knew she wasn't going to miss out on this opportunity.

Just as Keith was about to call it a night, he heard a light knock on the wooden screen door. He knew he wasn't expecting company. As he made his way over to the window, he peeked out. To his surprise, it was April standing on the front porch.

Now what could this country-ass girl want at this time of the night, he wondered. He knew he hadn't left anything in the truck. He opened the door and in walked April with a medium-sized duffle bag.

"Did I forget something?" asked Keith. He already knew the answer to his own question.

"No, you didn't. I think I have something you may need." April sat down on the outdated sofa and propped the black bag right next to her.

Keith paid close attention to her. He noticed April had changed into some tight jeans and applied makeup. He was too anxious to see what was in the black bag.

"So, are you going to tell me what's in the bag? I know you didn't come back here just because you want to come look in my face."

"Oh no, that's not the plan for me handsome. I have two fairly new twin 45 semi-automatic handguns in this here bag," she said, as she passed him the bag. "I sure hope I will be leaving this bag behind, only if you satisfy my burning fire, if you know what I mean," she said as she batted her eyes.

Keith wasn't slow to the proposition. It didn't take much convincing. He knew he needed a weapon to complete his mission. He wasn't about to miss this opportunity. And, to add icing on the cake, he got to smash a snow bunny in the process. He thought to himself, Hell yeah!

Chapter 18:
Curious Neighbor

Five months had passed since the Devin murder. No one knew who killed him. People did their usual speculation, but nobody knew for sure. Keith had just disappeared. No one had heard from hm. People continued asking his grandma, Mom Dukes, and she would normally say, "He's doing fine; God has him protected."

Old Man Wallace had the Southside on lock with the marijuana. Anything a customer wanted, he had it. The neighborhood didn't know he was the reason Devin was dead, but the hood also paid attention as well. He was no longer going around passing out hundred-dollar bills looking for information about who broke into his storage.

Many people in the neighborhood didn't want any static. They only wanted to do two things, sip their drink and smoke their good bud. And they knew for a fact Wallace kept that exotic.

Chapter 19:
Pay Back

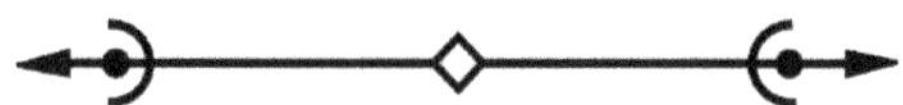

Keith had slipped back into town. He had been watching Old Man Wallace for a full week. He noticed Old Man Wallace no longer went out back to the storage house. He now drove to a house three houses down from his house. Keith realized that this was his stash house. He had figured the nigga out. He went to the stash house two times a day, in the morning and at night, he guessed, when he was turning in for the night.

Keith knew after that night that Old Man Wallace was going to be history.

Chapter 20:
Count Time

Wallace had run the bills he had made that day through the money-counting machine; it added up to be $14,500. He knew he had done pretty good for it to only be a Thursday. He took a sip of his Brandy and a hit of his Swisher Perfecto blunts. He looked down at his expensive George Daniels wristwatch and smoothed down his Armani suit. He had made plans to see with a high school teacher he had met a week ago. So, he carefully bagged the money up with the remaining two pounds of bud to put in the stash house.

He figured since time was winding down, he would walk instead of drive over to his stash house. As usual, he entered the quiet, dark house. He did as he normally would at the end of the night, entered the main bedroom, walked over to the closet where the safe was perfectly secured, and put his earnings in it.

Once the safe opened, Wallace was hit across his head with the butt end of a heavy-duty flashlight. He was out like a light. Keith frisked Old Man Wallace very thoroughly. He wanted to make sure he didn't have any type of weapon, especially a knife. Keith remembered the weapon that killed his boy.

Chapter 21:
Lights Out

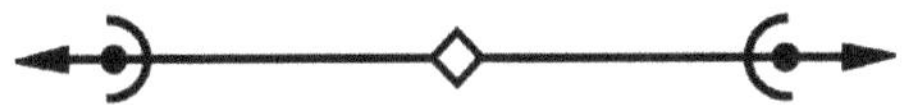

Forty-five minutes had passed, and Old Man Wallace was gagged and tied tightly down to a wooden chair in the middle of the kitchen. Keith was sitting a few feet from him, waiting patiently for him to gain consciousness. He just wanted to look the old nigga in his eyes before he took his life, since he took his boy's life.

As Wallace came back from the hard blow he took to the head, he opened his eyes. His vision was blurry, and he couldn't make out the individual that sat in front of him. He realized he was gagged and tied down to a chair.

"About time you wake your city slicker ass up," Keith said with a venomous tone.

"You just couldn't take the L and move on. You just had to even the score by trying to kill two country ass niggas. Those are your words, right? Safe to say you were successful with one kill."

Keith jumped up from his chair and went over and hit Old Man Wallace again with the heavy flashlight, knocking blood and teeth from his mouth. He knew if Old Man Wallace screamed that he would arrive to hell a lot sooner.

"I guess you thought I was going to run from you and never return. Huh? Did you really think I wasn't going to return, old motherfucker?" Keith asked as he pushed on Old Man Wallace's head with the flashlight.

"You are not a killer! Because if you were, I'd already be dead. Just stop kidding yourself. You better get your country-ass out my motherfucking house while you can, because if I get loose, I am going to do you worse than I did your crying-ass boy," Wallace said, as he spit from his bloody mouth.

"You're funny. And you're absolutely correct. I am not a killer, but tonight I will become one," Keith said as he pulled the chrome .45 from his waistband and put five hollow point bullets in Old Man Wallace's chest. "Now who's the country motherfucker?"

Chapter 22:
Chaplain's Office

"Big Bruh, the officer on the door want you," Lil Peanut said as he walked back to his bunk.

Keith looked down at his G-Shock wristwatch and realized that it was the next day. That bud had some major effects. As he rubbed the fog from his eyes, he made his way up to the control booth.

"You're needed in the chaplain's office," said the female officer.

"Are you sure they want Keith Rogers?" he asked in a confused manner.

"I believe you're the only Keith Rogers in this barrack," she said, while trying not to agitate him.

Keith walked away from the booth not sure how to take the information. He knew more times than not being called over to the chaplain's offices usually was bad news. He wasn't ready for bad news. He knew his mother wasn't at her best health. And from speaking with Mom Dukes, her health was declining, too. He had to get home and get there quick.

After Keith took care of his hygiene, he put on his creased down prison uniform and free-world Air Force Ones. He then removed the black doo-rag from his head. He looked in his hand-held mirror to see that his beehive waves were in place as he knew they would be. He reached into his hygiene bag and pulled out a bottle of Hugo Boss Cologne. He carefully poured a small portion in his hand, and rubbed some on his neck and down his uniform shirt.

As he walked out of the door to be pat-searched, the female officer, Corporal Digs, admired the scent and the neatness. "You do know you're only going to the chaplain office and not visitation," she said with a flirting tone while smiling.

"You might want to get used to this. This is my everyday look. To me, it's a major violation to be caught slipping looking bumish."

The other older female guard that worked across the hall from Corporal Diggs walked up to confirm what Keith was saying as the truth. "He's telling the truth girl. I've never seen him wrinkled," she said, as the old school officer gave him a head to toe look over.

Keith made his way over to the chaplain's office. As neared the office, he continued to repeat, "I hope my family is okay."

"Come in, Mr. Rogers, and have a seat," the black chaplain said, while extending his hand for a handshake.

After their handshake, Chaplain Burton got down to business. "I am afraid I have some bad news, Mr. Rogers." Keith looked on while waiting on the unwanted news. "Mr. Rogers, I am sorry to be the bearer of bad news, but this morning I received some disturbing information from a lady reporting to be your grandmother, Ms. Gladys Oliver."

"Yessir, that's my grandmother."

"I kind of figured that, especially after I looked in your file and saw where she's your emergency contact."

"Yessir, she is."

"She said that your mother's health has gotten extremely bad and the doctors are saying they do not see her pulling through the weekend."

Keith dropped his head while staring at the floor, not believing what he was hearing. His thoughts were distorted. It was already hard dealing with the fact he had been away from the two most important people he had in the entire world, but hearing his mother might not make it through the weekend was harder. Damn, he thought.

"Whenever you're ready, I will let you speak briefly to your grandmother. I believe you both need to hear from one another during a time like this."

"I'm ready, whenever you are."

"Is the number that's listed as your emergency contact the number Mrs. Oliver can be reached at?"

"Yessir." After the chaplain dialed the number, he soon exited the office.

"Hello," said Mom Dukes.

"Grandma, it's me, Keith," he said, as tears formed within his eyes. It had been over a year since he'd heard from either his mother or Granny.

"How have you been?" asked his grandmother.

"I've been maintaining. Staying out of the way."

"That's good to know. Sorry about the news."

"I know right. But how's my mom doing?" asked Keith, anxious to know how his mom's condition really was.

"Maybe about a month ago, she all of a sudden started having bad headaches. She just thought they were migraines. But come to find out she had a tumor on her brain. The doctors are saying the tumor has grown to an abnormal size."

"Forget what the doctors are saying. What do you think, Ma Dukes? Do you believe she's going to pull through this?" asked Keith, while getting agitated.

"Listen son, my faith is not in man. Psalm 118 verse 8 says, 'It is better to trust in the Lord than to put confidence in man.' So, if you are ready to see your mother walk out of that hospital better, then get on your knees tonight and tell God what you want and believe the things you're asking for have already come to pass."

Keith knew his Mom Dukes was very religious. He knew first-hand to take her at her word.

"Son, do you have a pen and a piece of paper available? I need for you to write these Bible scriptures down. Read them every day and pray a sincere prayer for your mother."

He grabbed the pen and notepad Chaplain Barton had on the desk. "I'm ready, Grandma."

"Proverbs 4:20-22, Psalm 103:1-5, Exodus 15:26, Deuteronomy 7:14-15, 1 Kings 8:56, and Psalm 91:14-16."

The chaplain walked back in to make sure everything was okay. Keith looked up at the chaplain as he walked back into the room. "Mom Dukes, I will do exactly what you asked of me starting tonight."

"Okay, my boy. I love you." The call ended.

"Mr. Rogers, when was the last time you went to church?" asked Chaplain Burton.

Keith knew it had been a while since he'd seen the inside of a prison church. He was so caught up in doing his own thing, to the point church was nowhere on his to-do list.

"To be honest with you, Chap, it's been awhile."

"Well tonight, I have some of my favorites coming in to worship with us. I would like to invite you out. Can I look for you?"

"Yessir, I will be here." He knew being in prison all a man had was his word. And plus, he knew he needed to be there anyway for the sake of his mother.

Chapter 23:
Staying Focus

As Keith paced his way back down the hall toward his barracks, his thoughts fell heavily on his mother and her condition. He knew for his entire life all he had were his mother and granny. The thought of losing either would be devastating. The only thing he could think of were the nine months he had left for the parole board, which wasn't coming fast enough. But he knew he had to do something to stay focused and try not to think of anything negative happening to his mother or Mom Dukes.

When Keith walked through the double doors of zone one, Corporal Diggs noticed the disturbed look on his face. She was new to the prison system; she knew she didn't want to say the wrong thing to agitate him. She just thought to say, when he made it to the barracks door, "Are you okay?"

Keith knew the environment he was in to be a dog-eat-dog world. Any sign of weakness, the vultures would come at you and attack. Too many people in prison didn't show sympathy for the next individual, unless that person had strong ties to the individual who was going through the hardship.

"For the most part, I'm going to be okay. Thanks for asking. To be honest, in this type of environment, you really do not get that from officers and especially from these rotten ass dudes that claim they're killers, drug lords, mocks, and even pimps, without having a hidden agenda. Truly, thanks."

"You know what, I hear that a lot and I've only been here on shift for a month now."

"Then you better take heed," he said, as he walked into the barracks, leaving the female officer with something to think about.

Once Keith made it to his bunk, Lil Peanut walked over to him with a fat marijuana joint rolled up, ready to start it up.

"Are you ready to get toasted?" asked Lil Peanut.

"Naw. I'm good, my boy. Do your thing. I got a lot on my mind right now," he said, as he laid back into his bunk in deep thought.

"Is everything alright?" asked a sincere and concerned Lil Peanut.

"Yeah, it's my T-Lady. Mom Dukes sounds as if she's not worried, but I don't know. That's her only child. She advises me to not worry and to put it in God's hand. But bruh, that's hard to do when the only thing you've ever done is take care of the things you need done your damn self."

"Bruh, I feel you, my boy. But let me ask you this. Is your Mom Dukes a religious woman?"

"Is she?" Keith repeated, as he pulled the piece of paper out with the Bible scriptures his granny gave him and held it up. "She wants me to read these verses every day and pray."

"My guy, you probably don't believe this shit, but I grew up in church. My old man was a deacon in the church, and my mom sang on the choir. So, I am not a stranger to God's house. If your Mom Dukes is anything like my mother and father, then I advise you to take her for her word and follow her instructions."

"Nigga, have you already been smoking before coming over here with that joint in your hand?" Keith said, as he and Lil Peanut started laughing.

"As I should! You know that bud you got is some heat. Of course, I had to wake and bake," he said, as they both did the Break Bread Forever handshake.

"The chap asked me to attend the church service tonight."

"So, are you going?"

"I gave him my word I would."

"Well, then enough said," Lil Peanut said as he pulled out his two AA Batteries and two broken razors to spark his joint.

"Are you coming with me?" asked Keith.

"I might tip over there with you, my boy. I hope there will be some females there. I may just get chose," Lil Peanut said, as he took a long pull from the joint.

"Boy, you're silly. But I feel ya!"

Chapter 24: Church Call

As the church building was filling up, in walked Keith, Lil Peanut, and another one of their guys making their way to the second row of pews. Several inmates who knew Keith, Lil Peanut, and K3 were surprised to see the men in church. But Keith knew he had a much bigger purpose for being amongst the worshippers.

The free-world visitors were singing a Kirk Franklin song that had most of the attendance standing with their hands held high praising the Lord. Keith and Chaplain Barton locked eyes as Barton gave Keith a head nod. The visitors were all from a black church. Keith thought to himself, by this being a black church, it just may get crunk. He was familiar with a Baptist church praise and worship service.

The middle-aged pastor took the podium and commended the men for coming out, leaving all the negativity behind and allowing God to transform their minds. He raised up his Bible and asked everyone there who brought one to do the same and repeat after him. Many people were looking around for a Bible. Keith held up his customized Bible his Mom Dukes gave him when he was going to the county jail.

Pastor Brown scanned the room with his eyes and said, "This is my Bible. This is my Lord speaking to me. I am what it says I am. I have what it says I have. I can do what it says I can do. Whatever God's word says, I believe it! I have it! It's mine! Hallelujah!"

"How many came out expecting a blessing? I didn't say looking for a blessing; I said expecting a blessing. There's a big difference between the two."

The church house was quiet. Pastor Brown had everyone's undivided attention. Keith's mind was on his mother. His grandmother's words were playing in his mind as he listened to the preacher speaking about healing.

"How many of you men have an illness or have a loved one who is dealing with an illness? Please raise your hand."

Keith couldn't get his hand up fast enough. He knew his mother needed a miracle, and he was willing to do just about anything to see his mother back to her normal self.

"The altar is open for you. Listen men, I know you may be sitting there wondering what your homies are going to think about you. Or how you are going to look after you leave the altar. Well, honestly, that shouldn't be something to concentrate on when you're a blessing from God. You know if you are dealing with a sickness, or have a family member who's fighting for their life, then you need to be at this altar. Praise God."

"Praise God!" The men in the church repeated.

As the preacher continued to speak, the men beelined their way to the front of the church. Keith didn't have to wait any longer; he stood up and made his way past Lil Peanut and K3. As he stood directly in front of the podium, he bowed his head as the preacher continued to invite the men to the altar. One of the prayer warriors who came along with Pastor Brown walked over to Keith to pray with him.

"How are you doing, young man?" asked an older, curly-headed man.

"Not so good," said Keith.

"What will we be praying for tonight?" asked the prayer warriors.

"My mom. The doctors are saying she might not live past this weekend," he said, as tears came rolling down his cheeks.

"The devil is a lie, young man. We're going to rebuke that in the blood of Jesus Christ."

The prayer warrior picked two of the females to surround Keith and put their hands on him as they prayed for him. Keith felt the power of God flowing through his body and throughout the church. As the deacon continued to pray over Keith, he could hear in the background, "I Surrender All" by Bishop T.D. Jakes playing softly. Something came over him. He felt the sensational feeling flow through his body. All he could think about was Mom Duke's wise words: "When the Holy Ghost power comes over you, you will know it. It's a feeling that's indescribable."

When the deacon finished praying, something within him assured him that his mother was going to be alright. But he knew he had to do his part as a believer. As he opened his eyes to return to his seat, he noticed everyone else was already back in their seats. He could tell Lil Peanut wanted to ask him a question once he returned to his seat, but he turned his head to disregard it.

Keith wanted better for his life. For the past twelve years, he'd been in prison for Old Man Wallace's murder. He managed to get caught by a hidden camera inside Old Man Wallace's house. A good Samaritan called the cops out for a welfare check on Wallace. People in the neighborhood became suspicious of his whereabouts, since they had not seen him in weeks.

After searching Wallace's residence and finding it empty, the nosy neighbors advised FCPD they should go over to his stash house. And as they guessed correctly, Old Man Wallace was in the house, still sitting in the same chair with several hollow point bullets in his chest.

As the cops investigated, they discovered that Old Man Wallace was on the run from Chicago, Illinois. Come to find out, Wallace wasn't his real name. His real name was Shawn Basemore. Back in Chicago, he was wanted for three murders, all of which had been committed with a knife. Once the detectives finished their investigation, it was determined that Old Man Wallace was Devin's killer. His house was searched and multiple butterfly knives were found. That appeared to be his favorite weapon to carry, since he had a collection of them and a security camera with stored video footage. The detectives saw Keith in the house killing Old Man Wallace. However, due to Old Man Wallace being on the run from Chicago for three murders and the murder of Devin Stacy, one of the detectives assured Keith's grandmother that her grandson wouldn't get much time in prison and that he would see the streets again.

Chapter 25:
Clowning Season

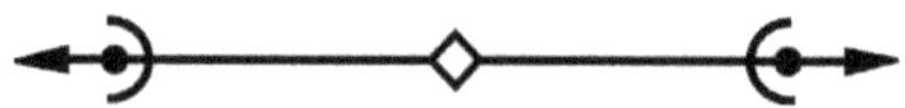

Ever since Keith found out about his mother's illness and that he could possibly lose her, he'd stopped smoking weed completely. His mind was focused on his main priorities: his mother, grandmother, and making the parole board. His homies thought he was taking his mother's sickness too seriously. He would always say to them, "Y'all might not love y'all people the same way I love mines, but when I heard the news about my T-Lady, I knew I had to do something different!"

Keith spent his time writing letters to LaSonya, working on his physique, and going over his plans for society. During his last three years, he'd spent that time hustling tobacco and weed. He'd manage to save $62,000. Luckily, he still had his bullheaded cousin he could depend on. They fought as kids but as soon as he went to prison, Shawna visited him once a month.

Keith's homies couldn't understand why he would stop hustling. He knew to quit while he was ahead. Lil Peanut understood the walk he'd chosen. K3 and the other guys (haters) didn't. They just thought he was acting brand new. They clowned him for not smoking marijuana and for attending church services. They teased him by calling him "church boy." He paid them no mind, because his mind was made up. If he wanted something different, he knew he had to do something different.

Chapter 26:
Gym Call

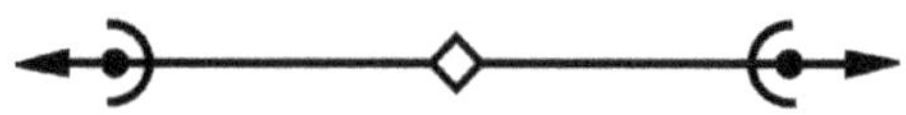

Keith took out his frustration on the punching bag or the speed bag at the gym, depending on which was not being used. He was good with his hands. Several suckers had tried testing his gangster and were carried away by their homeboys. For the past two weeks, he was under a lot of stress. He had realized the transition was harder than he thought. But he knew if he didn't make a change for the better, it was possible he could lose his mother and spend extra time in the hell hole.

He punched the bag with speed and great force. The other inmates looked on as Keith punched the bag in rhythm and style. Sweat dripped from his six-foot two frame. By beating up on the punching bag, he knew for sure the pressure would leave temporarily.

As he made his way back to his living quarters, Corporal Diggs stood at the barrack's door as each inmate returned from the gym. He had noticed how she asked more questions than usual and stood in the control booth of the barrack. She watched him as he moved throughout the barracks. He figured today would be the perfect time to ask her the question that had been swimming in his head for days.

"Miss Diggs, is there anything you would like to ask me, because I see you watching me from a distance all the time? I'm convinced already that you're not a cop. So, is there something you need to ask me?"

Her facial expression showed embarrassment. She stood there staring. She was in disbelief that he had noticed her careless admiration.

"I apologize for staring. I assure you I didn't mean anything by looking," she said, thinking that may have been enough to satisfy Keith's curiosity.

"Okay, you said all that to say what? You still haven't shared with me what's on your mind," he said as he stepped inside the barrack's waiting for her to speak her mind.

"Okay, since you want to know. As I look in each barrack I've worked, I've singled you out from the rest and viewed you to be different. Your swag is different. Your mannerism sticks out like a sore thumb. There's something about you that these other prisoners do not have. Just to be basically honest, I believe God has a calling on your life."

Now, Keith stood there in disbelief. He never expected to hear her say what he'd just heard. But he was a firm believer and knew it was a major violation to run out of conversation.

"That's interesting to know you have found me to be all that and some more. A person in my situation doesn't hear that too often. But thank you for noticing. Let me ask you a question. Do you believe in God?"

"Do I? He's the center of my life. All my life, I've been a part of a church. My father's a pastor and my mother is the choir director. And guess what?"

"What?"

"My father is still winning souls to this very day and my mother still has the church congregation praising the Lord."

"Is that right?"

"Very much so. I am a church baby," she responded, with the thought of her childhood upbringing making her laugh even harder.

Corporal Lakoiya Diggs reminded herself of the street rules her mother and father had when it came to church. It seemed like every time those church doors opened, she and her siblings had to be front and center. Keith's question took her from her strict childhood church rules.

"Miss Diggs, did I hear you correctly earlier when you said you've compared me to the other inmates here and noticed that I was different from them?" he asked while putting his Casanova suave charm down.

"That's correct. You did hear me say that loud and clear. Most of these dudes approach me with the lamest game they could possibly try to run on someone. And to make matters worse, their grooming be so weak."

"I know, right. Most of these young cats be on that young nigga mess, which means they hop up and let's go. Most of them are not focused on their appearance. And for the old heads, majority of them have given up."

"More or less, settle. Is that what you're trying to say?" asked Corporal Diggs.

"Well since you put it like that, I may have to suggest yeah."

"Mmm."

"Please do not get it twisted and think I'm the type to bash my fellow brothers, because that's not the case. Most of them do not see themselves as I see myself. My family principles have and will always be important to me no matter where I am. And that's big facts."

"Boy, you know you're funny. But I can respect that."

Someone from the back of the barracks called out Keith's name for his turn to shower.

"Sorry to cut our convo short, but I have to wash this sweat from my body. You know it's a must I stay so fresh and clean," he said, as he fast paced his way to the shower.

Chapter 27:
Quiet Storm

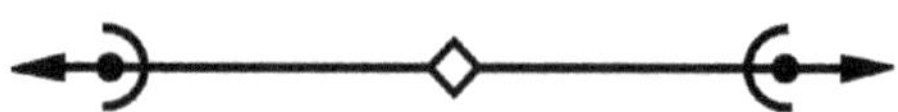

Keith sat at his bunk with pen in hand ready to bleed it as he listened to the new Drake song he'd purchased earlier that day. It felt weird to be sober. Normally when he wrote La Sonya a letter, he'd be on another planet mentally. He knew he was expecting something different, so he had to do what he knew to do. As the music quaked through his CL20 speakers, the vibe became surreal. He matched the energy by letting his thoughts flow on paper.

Friday, July 28, 2023

Dear My Goddess,

As always, I write this letter with the intent that it grabs your heart and not only squeezes it with a delicate squeeze but pampers it with the softness of a touch you could possibly feel.

I've sat around admiring the beautiful images I have of you. Having your pictures and inspiring words to captivate my focus have helped me decrease my thoughts from what I've had to bear these past few weeks.

You and others look in on my life and say, 'You're a strong individual to have endured the time of incarceration, the loss of your best friend, and now your mother is fighting for her life." I assure you all, only if you all knew. This has been tough, but every time a thought of defeat comes to mind, all I can hear is Mom Dukes saying, "Tough times don't last always, but tough people do."

As you know, I am a cognitive thinker, and by having the ability to think so deeply, I sometimes find myself asking the creator, "Why me?" Believe it or not, last weekend I asked that very question and while in prayer, the words became plain from a song I heard playing on the radio titled "Why not you?" Bae, that blew my mind. Again, I could hear Mom Duke's voice, as if she was right beside me say, "Trust God, Keith; He never abandons His children."

Things are happening more every day, to the point it's causing me to view Mom Dukes and your God in a different light. Out of nowhere, this older convict approached me just this week. He claimed he'd noticed my new walk and thought I needed a little encouragement. The words he spoke were straight to the point, but very impactful. "God didn't bring you this far just to leave you. You were designed with a purpose. Keep the faith, believer." And he walked away as smoothly as he came. And guess what? That was so weird, because I really did need some assurance that God was paying me some attention.

Please know your king is preparing himself mentally, emotionally, spiritually and not to brag, physically. You're going to love these washboard abs, lololololol…. I can see you now finding some kind of excuse for me to remove my shirt just so you can get a glance of my sexiness. Smile!

Allow me to share some good news as you, my T-Lady and Mom Dukes would call it. The chaplain of the unit came to me over two weeks ago and asked me to come before the church and give my testimony. I was stunned by the question. God was really testing my faith.

Bae, by having this question pop up on me, it took me back to a very familiar passage in the book of Jonah. I knew God was speaking through Chaplain Burton. Who am I to be dedicated to the calling of God? So sweetheart, by the time you read this letter, I've already given my testimony. So, pray for me.

As I end this letter, I always want you to know my thoughts of you are very strong. As intoxicating as your expression of love is, I am convinced I am filled until I hear from you again.

Peace and Blessings!

Sincerely,

Keith

Chapter 28:
Testimony

Keith thought as he walked into the gathering that there were more prisoners that came out to attend service than normal. Lecrae's song "I'll Find You" flowed through the speakers in the church. Keith found a seat in the front of the church, because he knew he would be called sometime before the service ended.

As he looked around the church, he noticed his old crew sitting to the left of him, looking as if they had just finished smoking. He had come to realize that it felt better to have joy. Something tugged at his heart with excitement for the decision he'd made by giving his testimony. He smiled at the thought if his Mom Dukes and T-Lady could see him now. Keith was taken from his thoughts by a nudge on the shoulder from the usher that stood beside him as he was getting his attention for the waiting chaplain.

"Church family, today there will be a very familiar face from your population coming forward to give his testimony. Please, by a standing ovation and hands of applause, let's recognize this brave and courageous young brother."

Chaplain Burton handed Keith the cordless microphone. As Keith walked upon the platform, he felt jitters throughout his body. He'd figured there was no turning back now. Now was the time.

"Good morning my comrades," he spoke comfortably.

Everybody responded by saying, "Good morning."

"Before I give my testimony this morning, I would like to lead us in prayer." He looked over at Chaplain Burton and was given the okay signal. "If you all would bow your heads and close your eyes as we go into prayer. Lord, I thank you for the rest You have given us and for allowing us to wake up to a new day. I pray for Your hand of protection for us and our loved ones. Give us grace and compassion in all that we do and say. Let us be a reflection of You, Lord, that others may desire to know the joy and contentment that lives within us. It is You who enables us to walk each day through what may come our way. And, Father, allow the words that come from my heart and mouth to be from you. Thank you. In Jesus Name, I pray. Amen."

"Amen."

"Again, good morning. Many of you here may know me already, but if you don't, then please allow me to introduce myself. My name is Keith Rogers. I am from a small but vibrant town, Forrest City, Arkansas. I was sent to prison for second degree murder and sentenced to twenty-five years. I've spent the last twelve years preparing myself for my freedom. Everyday has been a struggle. Many of you men understand when I say that."

"Amen to that brother," one of the guys said from the back of the church.

"At the age of 16, I found my best friend dead with his throat cut. He was like a brother to me. This really did affect me tremendously. My thoughts were distorted, and in my heart, all I wanted was revenge. And indeed, I did. Did that bring me peace? I guess, but I sometimes don't know. God has protected me more times than I can count. So, I can only imagine the times I've been rescued that I don't even know about."

As he looked over at his old homies, he knew he had their undivided attention because they had moved to the front pews.

"These past few months have been very trying. I was called into the chaplain's office for a bad news report. My Mom Dukes called and reported that my T-Lady was fighting for her life, and it wasn't looking too good for her. She even said the doctors…" he raised both of his hands up to show nonchalant hand gestures with his two fingers, "man," said she might not live through the weekend."

Keith looked up towards heaven and said, "God had a different plan for her life. Hallelujah!" The entire church stood up clapping and praising God. Keith's body was on fire. He knew he was now experiencing the Holy Ghost power. "My Mom Dukes gave me several scriptures from the Bible to read every day and pray over my mom's body. I assure you I did all of that. I was obedient. It's going on three weeks now, and my T-Lady is out of the hospital living her best life."

The congregation exploded in praises. "Praise God! Glory to God! I know you're able! Hallelujah!"

"Chaplain Burton called me down to his office in the earlier part of the week to relay a message from Mom Dukes. He saw the depressed look I had on my face when I walked in his office. He said, 'Young man, your grandmother wanted me to tell you that your mother went for her final CAT scan and nothing could be found.' Now y'all tell me, is there a God or not?"

Keith felt good. He knew Mom Dukes and T-Lady would be proud of him. As he walked off the stage, he noticed Lil Peanut and K3 were standing along with the entire church clapping their hands. He walked over to them both and showed them love by doing the Break Bread Forever handshake.

Chapter 29:
Parole Board

"Father God, today is another blessed day You have allowed me to see. I thank you for everything. God, I come humbly asking You to be with me as I go into this parole board interview. I ask You for the words to speak today. Please Father, do not let me stand in my own way. I decree and declare the things I've brought before You are already done. Thank you, AMEN!"

Keith stood after kneeling down beside his bunk. He felt this day would never come. It had been a long time coming. He knew only God had the last and final say for his release. Many prisoners tried to convince him to be prepared for a denial, due to the fact that he had a murder charge. But he refused to listen. He knew after he dedicated his life to God, the rest was history. He'd sincerely committed himself to follow the Lord.

"Inmate Rogers, they're ready for you in visitation for your parole meeting," said the male officer who was standing at the door waiting for Keith to make his way to the front of the barracks.

"Good luck Keith," said Lil Peanut.

"What's luck when I have God's grace," he said, as he turned to look at Lil Peanut and never broke his stride as he headed out of the barracks door.

An older white man with only two teeth in his mouth said as Keith was exiting the barracks, "You sure know what to say, young fellow."

"Well, there's no need of prolonging this interview. We might as well get this show on the road."

Keith's attention and focus were locked in on the man who was doing all the talking. Keith was nervous, but he was confident that God stood near him as he twirled his fingers in a circular motion underneath the table.

"Mr. Rogers, you were sentenced to 25 years for second degree murder. Is that correct?"

"Yessir."

"It shows you've been down for twelve years and nine months on this sentence."

"Yessir. Day for day," Keith added.

"As I look at your behavior history, I see you've had two major infractions during your twelve years of incarceration," the man said, looking up over his wire frame eyeglasses.

Keith was ushered in the small secluded room where the parole interview was being held by a female guard. When he entered the room, he was faced by a strong faced Caucasian male and a black female who appeared to be no more than thirty-five years of age.

"Hello," said the white man.

"Hello to you both," Keith said, extending his hand for a handshake.

"Will you state your full name and correctional identification number for us, please?" asked the male.

"Keith Rogers. My number is 111234."

"Okay, that's great. We wanted to make sure we have the right person before us today." The three found this comment humorous and laughed.

"Yessir."

"Do you care to elaborate for us, Mr. Rogers?"

He looked at their name tags on their coat jackets and politely said, "Mr. Wyatt and Ms. Phillips, I do not mind. When I first entered these prison doors, it was so chaotic and plus I was still a teenager trying to survive in a hostile environment. The very first day the new inmates walked in the prison, we were approached by several prisoners demanding to know our charges, where we were from and what type of personal property we had. One thing led to another, and a guy tried to take my commissary purchased tennis shoes and a Fossil watch. Mr. Wyatt, to be perfectly honest with you, I wasn't about to let that happen. My mother and grandmother remembered me as a man, and I had plans to return home as one. And the second incident basically didn't have anything to do with me.

"Due to the altercation and it being a race riot within the barracks I was assigned to, the officers gathered every black person and white male and separated us. They accused us of major disciplinary violations."

Keith watched the two while trying to read their body language as he told his story. He felt he was a good judge of character, but right now, he couldn't tell what to think.

"Okay Mr. Rogers, looking at your certificates, it shows you've achieved a GED, parenting class, thinking class, cognitive thinking class, SATP, anger management, PALS program, and the Leave No Man Behind Mentorship Program. I can tell you have tried to transition yourself for society."

"Yessir."

"Ms. Phillips, is there anything you would like to ask Mr. Rogers?" asked Mr. Wyatt as he looked at her.

"Sure. I have several questions for you, Mr. Rogers," she said, staring directly at Keith as if she was trying to penetrate his heart.

Again, Keith tried his best to read her body language to give him some kind of clue where he stood with their decision. Still, he was clueless.

"I heard you mention something about your mother and grandmother remembering you as a man and you had planned to return as one. Is that correct, Mr. Rogers?"

"Yes ma'am. I did say that."

"Mmmmmmh. Suppose that same incident were to happen on the day you're released from prison. So, you mean to tell my colleague and me that you would take matters into your own hands again?" Ms. Phillips spoke as if she saw him as a vindictive person.

"Ms. Phillips and Mr. Wyatt…"

They both had their eyes locked in on him waiting to hear his explanation.

"When I walked through those prison doors over twelve years ago, I thought and acted like a child. After interacting with these broken men and paying attention to their thinking, I realized I was a lot smarter than I gave myself credit for. Back then, I moved recklessly. My understanding wasn't what it is now. In reality, the majority of the people I grew up with as a kid are either strung out on drugs, or pushing up daisies. I truly thank God for grabbing my attention when He tried to keep me from falling victim like them. I am humbler now than I've ever been. And finally, I'll add, my grandmother and mother need me more now than ever. Their health is declining, and they both say all the time how they hear the maturity in my voice."

"Interesting, Mr. Rogers, and very convincing. But do you know how many times we hear that same sales pitch and within six months after their release, they return back with a new conviction?"

"I can only imagine. But I assure you both that won't be me. I can assure you both of that."

"How can you be so sure of yourself, that you're not going to return home and return back to prison in a few months' time or even some hours, Mr. Rogers?" asked Ms. Phillips.

"To be honest, I've worked for years to tell someone in your position of my plan to successfully stay home. For the past three years, I've had the opportunity to work closely with an intelligent young brother by the name of Kingdom Mason, who founded and started a mentorship program in this very prison for men. I've paid close attention to this brother, how he dealt with the men in the program. I know firsthand how to interact with broken individuals. Within the past three years, there have been over 350 prisoners to successfully complete this program. Over 300 of these men are still maintaining their class status and their sobriety. The whole while being a part of this unique program, I thought about my community back home."

"Is that right?" asked Ms. Phillips, while finding what he was saying to be very interesting.

"Yes ma'am. Over the last year, I've been designing a youth program." He opened his manila folder and removed three copies of the business plan for the youth program. He gave Ms. Phillips a copy and then handed Mr. Wyatt one as well. Keith continued his flow.

"The acronym for Youth is **Y**oung, **O**ptimistic, **U**nique, **T**ough, **H**eroes."

He paid attention to both of the parole officers as they shook their heads in agreement, familiarizing themselves with the plan.

"Mr. Rogers, I sense sincerity and determination within your conversation. I've listened to men one after the other, come before me with their best freedom speech and I've never been as convinced as I am today."

"Yessir," said Keith, giving his undivided attention.

"Mr. Rogers, ninety percent of the time the parole board members normally vote my way. Sitting here today listening to you speak, I am convinced that you will return home and become a productive citizen. Something just touched my spirit to give you a shot."

"Thank you, Mr. Wyatt. I assure you I do not plan to let you down," said a nervous but anxious Keith.

"Well, Mr. Rogers, there are five board members on the voting panel. It doesn't take but one to change the verdict of the vote. Three could vote for you or three could vote against you, then we could be seeing you next year. But to add to Mr. Wyatt's statements, ninety percent of the time the majority will vote his way."

"Ms. Phillips, may I ask you a question?" Keith asked, looking her squarely in the eyes.

"Sure. Shoot for it."

"Do I have your vote?"

"Yes, you do, Mr. Rogers," responded a Ms. Phillips, who smiled for the first time.

"Thank you both. May I be excused?"

"Yes, you may," said Mr. Wyatt.

"Officer Wilson, will you please escort the next prisoner in, please? Thank you," said Ms. Phillips.

Keith couldn't wait to share the good news with those near and dear. He knew it was a possibility that Shawna was ready to visit him that weekend. She would be the first to know. As he made it to his prison bunk, he removed his state uniform shirt, sat on his bed and bowed his head. He still couldn't believe what he had just heard. His thoughts were interrupted by J.M., the wise convict.

"Excuse me, young brother," said J. M, waiting to get Keith's attention.

"Oh what's up, O.G?" he asked, as he moved the small clutter of things to the side to allow J. M. to sit.

"I do not mean to pry into your business, but you're glowing my brother," J. M. said as he smiled.

"What do you mean, old school?"

"Young brother, it is written all over your face. Your facial expression is saying one thing, but your glow is showing the favor of God."

"Is it that obvious?"

"Having Godly eyes, you see with a spiritual vision, and I see a halo hovering over your head, son."

"You got to be kidding me," said Keith.

"I kid you not."

"Well, since it's that obvious, I guess I owe it all to God."

"Amen! But what kind of news did you receive from the parole board today?"

"I am gone. They both agreed to let me go," said a smiling Keith.

"Praise God."

"O.G. I was so nervous when I walked into that room."

"I can imagine."

"But I knew God was with me. I felt peace all over me." Keith was now experiencing the same feeling he felt when he was giving his testimony.

"Young brother, you have another chance to live a productive life. I advise you to take full advantage of this opportunity and go out there and live your best life. The sky's the limit. So, you know what that means, right?"

"Right. No limits."

"Do not let no one, not even yourself, trick you out of your spot. It's your time to go home and soar your wings as a young eagle would."

"O.G., that's my plan. I've had twelve years and nine months to prepare myself for my free world success. But on some real talk O.G., it's not about me anymore," he said with a serious face.

"What do you mean?"

"I am now 29 years old. In a few months, I will be a dirty thirty, as the old heads call it." They both found that to be funny. "I have people who need me to be the leader. So, I must put away my childish ways and grow up. Do what's expected of me."

"Right on."

"By this time next year, mark my word, you will be seeing me on the local news. I will be opening a brand-new youth facility in Forrest City, Arkansas, for my community. That's my word, O.G."

"Well, you have my blessing, young brother. There are two things I would like to leave with you, if I may?" he asked, as he looked at Keith and waited for a reply.

"Sure, what is it?"

"The first one is a prayer. May I pray for you as you get ready to start your journey on the outside?"

"Man, yeah. That's an understatement. God is the Head of my life. Let's pray," Keith said, as he and J. M. stood together while holding hands in their praying position.

"Our Father who's in Heaven, we join hands and connect as one, asking You to accept this humble prayer. Here's a young brother whose heart is open for Your love. He comes humbly and boldly seeking You to guide him from this day forward. Father, search his heart from anything that's going to rob him of glorifying Your Holy name. Please remove it from him. As he gets ready to re-enter society, patiently walk alongside this brother. May Your protection be what keeps him safe. May Your peace be what secures him in any unfamiliar environment. May Your love be what is satisfying to love as many people as You will have before him, to show the Agape love Your Son Jesus Christ showed when He died for our sins. Father God, cover his mind from being attacked. Allow him to see the vultures who hide behind their smiles. Thank You, Father God, for being a merciful God. We decree and declare that these words are accepted in the Kingdom of Heaven, Amen."

"Thank you, O.G.," Keith said, as he shook the old timer's hand.

"And last but not least, God will find you where you are. You can be in a bottomless pit when you call out to Him sincerely. My friend, He's coming. You have now been transformed from a thug to a saint."

"Right," Keith agreed, liking the sound of that. "From a thug to a saint. I like that, O.G."

"Now, will you show me how to do that cool handshake I be seeing you youngsters doing?" asked J. M.

"Oh, you referring to that 'Break Bread Forever' shake. You do your fist like this. You bump my thumb with your thumb, and you break it, and open your hand as if you are spreading crumbs for the birds, while saying 'Break bread forever. Crumbs everywhere.'"

"Curious. What do 'crumbs everywhere mean?'"

"The crumbs are opportunities that a person has if they only have the mindset and vision to understand them."

"I like that, young brother. May we do it again?"

Chapter 30: Inquiring Mind

"Inmate Keith Rogers, you're needed down at the Master Control Center," said Sgt. Walker.

Keith was on the lay-in to see the institutional parole officer at the unit. As Keith waited on his turn to speak to the parole officer in the unit library in a single file line, all he could think about was his release day. It seemed like forever for him to get to this point. He had already informed his big-headed cousin of the day he was to be released. He wanted her to bring him black 501 Levi Straus jeans, a black Ralph Lauren Polo shirt with the red polo logo, and some of his favorite black, red, and gray Air Max 95's tennis shoes. His thoughts were interrupted by Mr. Griffin, the parole officer.

"Inmate Rogers, please step forward."

He shook the thoughts and stepped forward.

"Mr. Rogers, you're here today to fill out your release papers," she said, as she slid him several pieces of paper along with a black ink pen.

"Yes ma'am."

"As I have informed the men before you and I am informing the men after you, if you're not for sure about your family or whoever you've told to pick you up next Monday, then you need to let me know by the end of the week. That way, I can make arrangements to have you dropped off at the bus station in Little Rock, Arkansas. So, do you have a for sure ride home, Mr. Rogers?" she asked, looking up at Keith and waiting for his answer.

"Yes ma'am. I have someone. Matter of fact, I need you to find this out. The day I am to leave, what will happen to the money that's on my prison account?"

"For anyone who has funds on their prison accounts, you have nothing to worry about. All your funds will be added to your release debit card. Anything else?"

"No ma'am."

"Find you a seat at one of those tables over there as I attend to the rest. Mr. Mason, will you step forward, please?"

Keith found a seat at an empty four-man table, anxiously ready to fill out his release papers. The time had finally come for what he'd envisioned since the day he entered prison. He looked up from finishing his release packet and noticed several guys huddled and pointing at their papers. He was too sure of the required information he'd written down on his papers. All he needed was the exit door.

"Okay gentlemen, if you know you've filled every line out correctly and don't have any more questions, then will you please bring me your packet? But if you're unsure of some of the information that is required, then stand over there in a single file line." Ms. Griffin pointed to her left.

Keith and three other men walked over to Ms. Griffin's table and handed her their completed packets and exited the unit library. Keith knew it was downhill from that point on. He knew he had to remain focused for six days and a wake up.

As Keith was heading back to his barracks from the unit library, Sgt. Walker, the hall sergeant, told him that the officer down 15 Barracks wanted to see him. He scrolled up the hallway feeling like he was on top of the world. As he walked past the other barracks, the inmates that Keith had done time with knocked on the windows speaking, showing him love as they did when seeing someone they knew. Before he made it through at least three double doors, he saw Corporal Diggs standing outside 15 Barracks.

"What's up lady," said a smiling Keith, showing his bright, white smile.

"Nothing too much. I just wanted to check on you. I haven't been working your barracks, and I haven't been seeing you in the hall as much. Are you straight?" asked a smiling Diggs.

"You know how I rock. I deal with a few and when I deal with them, it's strictly business. Point. Blank. Period."

"That's what's up. But how did the parole hearing go? Are you on your way home?"

"I'm going to say it like this; you're looking at a free man," he said, smiling.

"Are you serious?"

"Serious as a heart attack."

"What's your plans upon release?" asked Diggs, trying not to sound too excited.

"First and foremost, it is a must I go home and see my T-Lady and Mom Dukes."

"What female you have waiting for you? And don't lie!"

"Are you asking the question, hoping you will be the one I call or you're just being nosey?"

"Boy, you're funny," she said, still avoiding the question.

"I've been told that a time or two. But I still haven't heard you answer my question," he said as he looked at her.

"To be honest with you, I've found you attractive from the first time I worked at your barracks. You are my type of man I will date in the free world," said an honest Diggs.

"Thanks for the compliment," he said while smoothing down his waves. "In reality, I'm really flattered sweetheart, but to be honest with you, I have someone."

"OMG! I feel silly."

"You shouldn't. Mom Dukes has always said a closed mouth won't get fed. You just spoke your mind and pursued what you wanted. There is nothing wrong with that," he said, dissuading her from feeling embarrassed.

"Look at you, trying to downplay my silliness." She smiled.

Keith walked up closer to her, not trying to invade too much of her space. "Just because I am with someone doesn't mean it's illegal to have a friend."

"A friend."

"What's wrong with having a friend? Someone that your mate knows about and you and that person even go out for lunch or something," said Keith trying not to laugh.

"In what fantasy world are you living? No one these days and times is with no Fantasy Island mess like that anymore, if ever."

"What do you mean? So, you mean to tell me if the shoe was on the other foot and you were my lady, and I told you, 'Bae, I am going to have lunch with a female friend,' you will get bent out of shape over a friendly, lunch date with a female friend?"

"The only thing I will be telling you is, add another chair to this dining table, because I would be right there enjoying an appetizer while you and your female friend enjoy y'all lunch."

"Are you serious, now?"

"Do you see my face? I am not smiling, and that's big facts!"

"Well, I guess that killed that thought."

"Well, I guess it has, too," she said nonchalantly.

"Now you're funny," he said, being serious.

"Well, Mr. Free World, I'm not going to hold you up. Just make sure you take care of yourself and try your damnest not to come back to prison. You have too much potential. Go out there and make it work for yourself. As Jeezy says, "The sky is the limit.""

"No doubt, Ms. Diggs. Thanks for the advice," he said, as he turned around, making his way back to this barrack.

Chapter 31:
Keith's Faith Tested

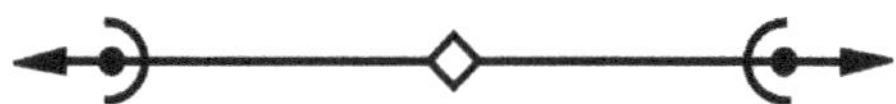

As Keith walked into the crowded dining hall, he was sure every inmate came out to eat that day. Fried chicken, macaroni and cheese, string beans, black eyed peas, peanut butter cake with peanut butter icing, and sweet iced tea were being served for lunch. As always, the entire staff had their section to watch, making sure the inmates did not double back for seconds.

Keith, having been imprisoned for over twelve years and once being a hustler, he was well known to the prison population. As he made his way to the meal slot to grab his lunch tray, he thanked the food supervisor, Ms. Bryant, for preparing another edible meal. He found a table with one person sitting there. He looked around the dining hall and saw a lot of contraband transactions going on, even though there were staff members not even five feet from where they conducted their business underneath the tables.

As he finished up with his last bite of peanut butter cake, an officer stopped beside him, bent down and picked something up from the floor. He paid it no attention because it didn't have anything to do with him. As he made his way to the dish room window, he was stopped by a guy he knew from his hometown.

"What's up my boy? I heard you made the parole board," he said, as the two did the Break Bread Forever handshake.

"Ah, what's up homie? I did, my boy."

"I know you're glad," said Champ.

"'Glad' is an understatement. Bruh, I'm so ready to leave this madness," Keith said, as he looked around the dining hall.

"I feel you, Bruh. Stay up my boy. I'll be out soon. Try to save me some of those big booty ladies," he said, as they did their handshake again before parting ways.

Just as Keith was getting ready to walk through the metal detector, the captain and the sergeant he saw bending down to retrieve whatever was on the floor, approached him, demanding him to turn around to be placed in handcuffs.

"What's the matter, captain?" asked Keith, who was confused about being placed in handcuffs.

"My officer said he saw some contraband fall from your pocket."

"I assure you, captain, he's mistaken."

"So, are you calling my officer a liar, convict?" the captain asked, while turning red in the face.

"Well, to be honest, he's mistaken. Because he did not see me drop anything from my pocket at any time."

Keith was ushered down to the holding cell in front of the infirmary. His mind was racing a hundred miles per second. He couldn't believe his faith was being tested like this.

He paced backwards and forwards in the small, cold holding cell. His thoughts were somewhat distorted at this point. He couldn't understand how this could be happening to him, and now. He was only five days and a wakeup away from becoming a free man. All kinds of thoughts attacked his mind. Satan was trying to plant seed after seed in his mind. But he continued to say to himself, "God has a plan; I must trust him."

As the inmates filled the hallways heading east from the dining hall, Keith could hear their remarks. They gave their opinions of the reason he was being locked up.

"I knew that nigga was still hustling."

"Naw, Bruh don't hustle anymore; he gave his life to God."

The next person could be heard saying, "Once a hustler, always a hustler."

"God, I am glad they are not you," he said in a low whisper.

30 Minutes Later

The lock popped on the holding cell door, and in walked two sergeants, the one that claimed he saw Keith drop the contraband from his pocket and a female.

"Are you letting me go back to my barracks," asked Keith, trying not to sound agitated.

"Well, not quite. The captain wants to investigate this matter," said the sergeant.

"What is there to investigate? Point, blank, period. I didn't drop that whatever you supposedly picked up from the floor."

"Calm down, Inmate Rogers," said Sgt. Bell, as she continued.

"Turn around so I can place you in handcuffs so you can be escorted down to the east building. You're only under investigation."

"Sgt. Bell, this is wrong. I never had whatever he's trying to say is mine. What it look like for me to have some contraband when I've made parole and I'm leaving Monday morning? That does not make sense."

"I've seen plenty of you guys throw their chances of going home away for something that is worthless," said the male sergeant.

"Sir, what is your name? I will be praying for you. Everybody is not the same."

"Sgt. Petty. And that's with a capital P-E-T-T-Y. Make sure you tell your God I need a raise. Now let's move it, Mr. Rogers," he said in a smart aleck tone.

As Keith was given the standard procedure of the pre-lock-up protocol and escorted to the east building, his anger continuously progressed. He still couldn't believe God was allowing this to happen to him at a time like this. As he was escorted down the hallway, inmates on both sides of the hall knocked on their window either to be nosey or share their empathy.

"Mr. Rogers, if you know for a fact that what was found is not yours, stand on what you believe in. Don't get discouraged. Trust God. Like I said, it's only an investigation for now. The captain said he would investigate the matter, then expect that to happen," said Sgt. Bell, as they locked Keith in an isolated cell.

Chapter 32:

Investigation

Day One of the Investigation

With its uncomfortable living conditions, constant noise, and unpleasant people, isolation was dark and lonely. Keith laid awake on his back, locked in on a dot that was on the ceiling. He listened to the other inmates who were locked in their cells shout at one another all day and all night long.

Keith tried to reason with himself that everything was going to be alright. But that evil spirit always spoke differently. He couldn't eat. He couldn't sleep. All he did was pace the floor. He tried reading his Bible but something wouldn't let him keep his focus. He even tried doing push-ups to relieve his frustration, but he couldn't muster the energy to do ten. He was depleted.

Finally, he dropped down to his knees, throwing his hands in the air, looking up to the ceiling, and calling out to God.

"God, here I am, at my lowest. It is in a bottomless pit seeking You for mercy. I call out to You asking You to intervene in this cruel situation. You know my heart God. If there's anything I have not fully let go of, will You please remove it from me? Search my heart, Father. You are the Head of my life. I am now sold out to You. I pray You see what's going on and show me favor. Amen."

Day Two of the Investigation

Isolation was like a dry, parched land, and an individual soul thirsted for water. Keith was on lock down for 23 hours a day, only allowed out a few times a week for a shower and recreation. He had plenty of time to talk with and listen to the Lord with no distraction. He'd found the concentration he needed to study God's word. The isolation drew his relationship even closer to God, and eventually he recommitted his life to Jesus. He became the friend he needed most.

It didn't take long for the stories he had enjoyed when Mom Dukes encouraged him to read as a child to come alive and revive his spirit, and he began to notice a common thread in the lives of his Bible heroes. They were all deeply flawed people with epic moral failures, just like him, yet they were never out of reach of God's love, grace, and mercy.

As he paced that stained and worn-out tile, he remembered how Moses had killed an Egyptian and fled to the wilderness, but God still called him to lead the Nation of Israel out of captivity. King David committed adultery and murder, but when he repented, God forgave him. And scripture calls him a man after God's own heart. Saul murdered Christians, until he met Jesus on the Damascus Road and became the Apostle Paul, a great missionary for Christ.

Even though Keith was being reminded of God's love for His firm believers, the enemy still tried depriving him into not believing God's promises. But Mom Duke's sweet voice could only be heard: "Tough times don't last, but tough people do."

Day Three of the Investigation

Sweat dripped from Keith's body as he finished a fifty- count set of burpees, Sgt. Bell and Sgt. Guns stood in front of his cell with a size eight, one-piece jumpsuit. "Inmate Rogers, we're here to escort you to the captain's office," said Sgt. Bell.

"Okay, give me just a second to wipe myself down," he said, as he stood in front of the two female guards using the drying towel. Minutes later, he was escorted into the captain's office. As he walked into the office, he saw a familiar face, Chaplain Burton. He gave Chaplain Burton a head nod and faced Captain Crawford, giving him his attention. The female sergeants stood to the side as Captain Crawford started to talk.

"I've done my three-day standard investigation concerning the contraband incident in the kitchen. I tried pulling up different angles from footage from our camera system and was unsuccessful. Several people, such as

Chaplain Burton and these two sergeants right here spoke on your behalf that you are not the kind of inmate to chance your parole over some contraband."

Nothing but excitement was running through Keith's entire body. He felt as if he'd just hit the jackpot. "Thank You God," he whispered under his breath.

As Keith was thanking the chaplain and the two sergeants, Sgt. Bell released him from the handcuffs. "If I knew I wouldn't get locked back up, I promise you, I would hug you all," Keith said, as he rubbed his wrist from where the handcuffs once were.

"A thank you and a handshake will do young man," said Chaplain Burton, as he stood up to shake Keith's hand.

"Thank you, Captain Crawford. Am I free to go get my property from isolation?"

"Yes, you're free to go."

Chapter 33:
Hello Free World

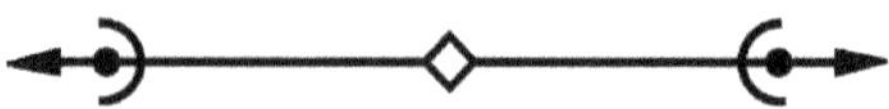

As Keith walked through the front entrance of the prison to leave, he spotted his bullet-headed cousin Shawna, Mom Dukes, T-Lady and LaSonya standing in the parking lot waiting for his arrival. Everyone squeezed in to give him a group hug.

Once the hug ended, Keith looked up to the sky, stretched out his hands and said, "God, I am free. Use me as you please. Thank You for saving me." He then hugged each one individually, giving every single one a kiss on the cheek. But he got very personal and graphic with LaSonya by giving her a passionate kiss.

"Big head, boy y'all need a hotel room for all that," said Shawna, as she started to laugh. As he looked around at the people he knew and loved unconditionally, a pain moved through his heart because his brother from another mother, Devin, was not there. He knew he had to make every move in remembrance of his boy. It was still hard for him not to blame himself for making better decisions before Devin's life was taken.

As they rode up the highway, the SUV was filled with laughter and conversation. Keith's mind was everywhere. He looked out the window thinking about the tough task he had in front of him. He remembered when he left the world, he was only a teenager who barely lived. Now, he was returning as a grown man who was considered the leader of his family.

"Grandson, it's going to be okay. God has already worked it out for you. All He needs for you to do is trust and believe," said Mom Dukes.

A single tear fell from Keith's eye. And he whispered, "Thank You, God, for Your assurance."

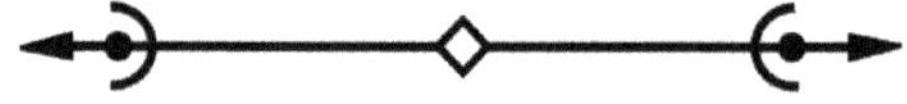

Wise Words from The Author

An attitude of gratitude doesn't happen naturally, especially in prison. When I wrote this book, I was in isolation at North Central Unit Prison in Calico Rock, Arkansas.

The heart of every prisoner is a battleground for the war between good and evil that surrounds them on a daily basis. Satan thrives on negativity that exists behind the razor wire. He works hard to keep the prisoners' attention on life's difficult and unpleasant circumstances, so they become critical and complain and turn away from God. Satan knows that if a person is looking only at what's wrong in their lives, they're bound to get depressed and succumb to hopelessness.

During the 16 years I have been locked up, I have learned the importance of living with gratitude, but it wasn't until I surrendered my life to Christ and started reading my Bible. I realize how much I have to be grateful for, even in prison.

No matter where your Google Map shows you to be, God is one click away. Peace and blessings, my friend.

Acknowledgments

First, I acknowledge God (for saving my life), my mother, Annette, my father, Freddie, Sr. (rest in Heaven), my brothers, Andre', Nicholas, and Freddie, Jr., my sisters, Nakisha, Niesha, and Tameka, my daughter: Kelis, my special friend, Dorothy, and to the people who prayed for me while I've been on this journey. Thank you.

I would like to send a special thank you to my publisher, Dr. Sonia Cunningham Leverette at Hadassah's Crown Publishing. Thank you for believing in my work.

And to the people who removed themselves from my life, I thank you for *not* staying during my trying times.

No matter what part you played in my life, I want to thank you.

R.I.L. Kendrick 'Ken' Rogers

R.I.L. Demetrius 'Pac-Man' Tripp

"Trust in him at all times; ye people, pour out your heart before him: God is a refuge for us." Psalm 62:8

Pulaski County Deputy Prosecutor Leigh B. Patterson

From a Thug to a Saint II Coming Soon

www.ingramcontent.com/pod-product-compliance
Lightning Source LLC
Chambersburg PA
CBHW061107100726
47911CB00012B/439